Chapter One

"Catch me if you can!"
The childish laughter rose in the cool
morning breeze. Lydia Thompson laughed
as she watched as the children frolicked
around the yard of the one-room
schoolhouse. Oh, to be so young and care
free once again! She turned from the
window and sighed. With the terrible war
going on, there wasn't too much to smile
about lately.

Her gaze fell to the small picture she
kept propped up on her desk next to her
Bible. Alex's boyish grin stared back at
her. Alex Thorne, the one she loved
above all else.

A lone tear streaked its way down her
cheek, and fell, unbidden, onto her
dark, navy dress followed quickly by
another. While his sweet smile reminded
her of the happier times they had
together, the crisp, new uniform he wore
spoke only of the sadness, and horror he
was now facing in an unforgiving war.

Lydia stifled a sob, and dropped into
the wooden chair behind her small,
wooden desk. "God, when will this war
ever be over?" she cried." Please be
with Alex, and keep him safe. Bring him
home to me. Amen".

"Are you alright, Ms Thompson?"
Lydia looked up into a pair of worried

brown eyes. Seven years old Amber Wright gazed up at her with a worried look on her face.

"I'm fine, Amber" Lydia forced a smile, and wiped away the remnants of her tears. She stood as the rest of the children entered, and started her class, as she always did, with a prayer

"God keep us in your eternal hand-Guide us, protect us, be with us...Amen"

A giggle interrupted in the back. Lydia glanced back, and followed fifteen year old Amy Wainwright's gaze across the crowded school house to sixteen year old Kevin Morgan. Oh, to be so young...so carefree...

Her memory slowly carried her to a much happier time...Had it only been three and a half short years ago?

It was Christmas 1914. Despite the fact that most of the world was now at war, the Thompson house once again resounded with laughter at this festive time of year.

Uncle Herb, and Aunt Bertha were visiting from Toronto, and with them came their two darling children, Liz, and Louie as well as tales of life in the big city.

Lydia loved Christmas! Although she was already eighteen-an old spinster as her cousins liked to call her-she still enjoyed the wonder of it all. The house was filled with the smells of freshly cut garlands, sweet scented pinecones, and wonderful aromas drifted from the oven as her mom, Mabel Thompson, did her Christmas baking.

It was Christmas Eve, and Alex was coming to pick her up for the evening service with his family's sleigh. Her heart sang with joy at the thought of seeing him once again. Who would have thought she would be this excited about seeing Alex? She had hated him so very much as a child!

She giggled as she thought of how he had made her life miserable-from yanking on her pigtails to dropping a frog into her lap, to filling her lunch box with worms. Alex had caused her many tears during her childhood, but the years had been kind.

Alex had grown into a handsome young man of nineteen. He was everything she wanted in a man. He loved God, and served him wholeheartedly. He was kind, caring, and compassionate.

She loved him.

That was what made it so complicated.

Alex urged the horses forward down the winding road to the Thompson farm. Snowflakes were softly falling, and yet there was a certain peaceful stillness in the air around him. There was no doubt that they would have a white

Christmas if this continued.

The candles in the window of the big white farmhouse broke into view. The door cracked open, and a small figure stepped out into the snowy night. His breath caught in his throat.

"Lydia."

Lydia, the girl he had come to cherish with all his being. Lydia was the one person who made sense in this war-ravaged world. Lydia whom he loved, but never found the courage to declare it.

And tonight he would break her heart.

Lydia adjusted the woolen cape around her shoulders, and stepped out onto the veranda. The jangling of bells filled the air, and she couldn't suppress the smile that threatened to spread its way across her face.

"Alex."

He pulled the sleigh up beside the porch, and helped her into it. After tucking a warm crochet blanket around her, he resumed his spot beside her, and together they rode towards their small country church.

Lydia gazed at this man beside her, and felt her heart flutter. How she loved him!

He put his arm around her, and she leaned against him. The snowflakes fell softly around them. It was a perfect night. She wished she could stay here forever.

They pulled into the church and parked
their sleigh next to the dozen or so
other sleighs and wagons already parked
at the little country church. The sound
of the organist warming up slowly
fluttered out the window as the glorious
strains of Oh Holy Night played loud and
strong added to the magic of the night.
Alex escorted her towards her family's
pew near the front of the church as the
pastor stepped to the pulpit.
    "Let us stand and worship the Christ
Child together"
    As the glorious refrain of Oh Come Let
Us Adore Him slowly faded, Alex turned
to Lydia, and hand-in-hand they walked
out into the night

How can I tell her? Alex wrestled
with his thoughts for about the
hundredth time that day
    How can I let her go? There was no
way around it, it had to be done.
    Slowly, he turned the sleigh towards
the lake. Couples skated in circles,
arms linked, and children laughed with
delight as they chased each other across
the icy surface

Lydia watched the wintry scene before her with childlike fascination. She loved winter, and all the beauty that came with it.

"Lydia"

Alex's whisper broke through her thoughts. She turned to him, and the look in his eyes took her breath away.

Tonight was the night! Tonight he would tell her he loved her, that he wanted to marry her, raise children with her...

"Yes?"

"We can't see each other anymore, Lydia."

"What?"

Never in her wildest dreams did she see this coming. Tears stung her eyes as she searched his soul for some explanation. She knew he loved her-she saw it in his eyes a moment ago as he looked at her.

"Why, Alex, why?"

Alex looked up into the tear-stained eyes, and his heart broke. Couldn't she see how hard this was for him? He found it best to be frank...

"I've joined the Army. I leave right after Christmas."

She looked at him stunned. She didn't

say a word, so he continued.

"I think it best we go our separate ways. Some men may be willing to ask a girl to wait for him, but you deserve better."

"No!" Lydia's look of determination shattered the last bit of resolve he had left. "I love you Alex Thorne! And I don't care how long I have to wait. I would wait for all eternity if I had to!"

Her tear-stained eyes pleaded with him until he could take it no more. His arms wrapped her in a warm embrace, and his lips found hers.

"I love you, too, Lydia. I love you with all my heart."

The love shone in her eyes, and he dared to press on

"Lydia Thompson, will you marry me knowing I am going out into this war, and may never return?"

She didn't hesitate for a second.

"I would be honored to be your wife."

Chapter Two

The deafening roar of the battlefield was enough to drive anyone mad. The shouts of men as they marched bravely on mingled with the anguished cries of the unfortunate souls as they breathed their last. The stench of death was everywhere. And still the war lagged on.

Would it never end?

Alex gazed around at the carnage around him. Where was God in all of this? Was He content to just sit by while the innocent were ravaged, and killed, or did He have a Plan in all of this heartache?

The tunnels were a wretched place to be, yet they provided some shelter from the seeming endless barrage of bombs, and gunfire. The conditions were terrible, the filth unbearable.

Yet even in all this wretchedness, Alex still held onto the one piece of beauty that remained in this hateful world. He took off his helmet, and ran his fingers over his short, dark hair. His gaze fell on the small black and white photograph he kept hidden deep inside his helmet.

"Lydia."

Even saying her name in a place like this seemed indecent. Her beautiful dancing eyes shimmered back at him.

He thought back to the night-three and a half years before-when he had proposed.

He'd had every intention of breaking it off with her to save her the heartache, but she would have none of it. He smiled, that was his Lydia. Determined, strong, the love of his life.

"What is that, buddy? A photograph of your girl back home?"

Alex glanced up to see Corporal Chuck

MacIntosh who gave him a good-natured slap on the back.

Chuck was Alex's closest friend.

Born in Toronto, Chuck was an only child. When his father had died from a freak accident when Chuck was 12, Chuck and his Mom were left all alone in the world.

They had struggled with poverty, and had overcome. They purchased a modest home in the suburbs of Toronto, and opened their hearts, and home to others who found themselves in the same conditions.

Then the war had started, and Chuck had been one of the very first to enlist. He believed in the cause, and was an honorable, brave, and courageous soldier.

Chuck was also one of the best Christians Alex had ever known. Out here, amidst all of the insanity, Chuck had held onto his faith, and let it shine like a candle flickering against the backdrop of a dark, black night.

While Alex liked conversing with his good friend, Chuck, he didn't particularly enjoy being pulled back to the present. No, he was content to sit there, and relive a better, happier time. A time with the woman he loved...

"Wish I had a girl like that waiting for me" Chuck said wistfully.

Alex laughed as he placed his helmet back on his head, "Someday, my friend, someday."

Suddenly, a flash lit up the sky above

them. Somewhere nearby, a bomb exploded. But it was much too close. Shrapnel fell everywhere, spreading destruction in it's path.

Screams filled the air as searing pain racked Alex's body. It was then that he realized the screams he heard were his own. Slowly, mercifully, he faded out of consciousness.

Lydia slowly rose from behind her desk at the little one-room schoolhouse. It was nearly the time to dismiss her class. She lifted her head at the sound of galloping hooves, and looked out the window as her father, Morgan Thompson, swung down from the saddle of his favorite black mare.

"Class, you are dismissed. I will see you all on Monday. And don't forget your assignments." A collective groan resounded through the classroom at the mention of the much-dreaded homework assignments.

Lydia waited until the sound of the rush of the children's feet to their weekend reprieve faded, and then walked to the door.

Her father met her on the front step, and handed her a crinkled yellow envelope. With shaking hands, she slowly opened it and dared to read the unfamiliar writing.

"Ms. Thompson: My name is Corporal

Chuck MacIntosh. I fought alongside Corporal Alex Thorne."

Lydia's eyes blurred. Why would this man be writing to her? Unless-no!

She dared not think of the horrible things that might have occurred. She turned and walked through the doorway, and slumped into the seat of the nearest desk. Her hands trembled as she read:

"Alex was injured two nights ago by shrapnel from a nearby bomb. We don't as of yet know the extent of his injuries. If I learn more, I will let you know. Sincerely, Chuck"

Lydia's eyes welled up with tears as she read, and reread the short letter before passing it to her father. She wished she knew more.

Was Alex severely wounded? Was he maimed, or crippled like many of the boys whom the war returned these days? Was he even now lying in a shallow grave in that unforgiving land with only a small white cross to forever memorialize him?

She would not, and dared not to think such things. A sob caught in her throat, and the tears flowed freely.

Comforting arms wrapped around her. All at once, she was six years old crying over a scraped knee. She had turned to her dad then as well.

"Don't cry" Morgan said as he gave his daughter a fatherly hug "Everything will be alright. God is still in control. He sees Alex, and only He can intervene..."

Her father's head bowed as he began to

pray, "God, be with Alex. Give him the healing, and the strength he needs. Bring him home to us once again. Amen."

Lights flickered overhead as Alex resumed consciousness.

He'd been having the strangest dream. He saw Lydia, her face radiant, standing at the altar in a beautiful white gown. Her gorgeous, dark hair was swept back, but a few loose curls had escaped. Her eyes sparkled, and a beautiful smile lit up her face.

Lydia was the most beautiful woman he had ever seen. How he loved her! And, now, today, and forever, she would be his.

Alex reached out to her.

"Lydia" he breathed.

Then he saw it.

She held an armful of brilliant red poppies.

Suddenly, a shadow covered the sparkle in her brown eyes, and tears streamed down her cheeks.

"Alex, come back to me!" She cried out in anguish.

He reached for her once again, but the scene began to blur.

It was only then that he realized she was standing there at the altar alone...

"No!" Alex cried out as the dream faded into reality. He could still hear the cries of anguished men, but the sounds of the bombing and gunfire had ceased.

As his vision came into focus, he saw two nurses leaning over him. Their faces looked grim.

"Am I going to die?" He asked as pain racked his body.

One reached down and patted his arm, "Of course not, corporal." It was meant to be a comfort. Instead the truth in her eyes belied her words.

As the nurses turned away to resume their rounds, the pain overcame Alex once again. Slowly, his vision blurred as he once again faded into the merciful darkness

---

Chapter Three

It was ten days later when Alex awoke.

As his vision came into focus, he looked up into a pair of mischievous, green eyes.

"It's about time, old buddy"

"Chuck" He forced a smile.

Corporal Chuck MacIntosh grinned, and motioned to a nurse that was passing by.

"Our pal over here has finally woke up. I told you he was a fighter."

A smile made it's way across the weary face of the young nurse. She leaned over Alex's bed, and felt his forehead.

"So he has. And his fever has broken. It's a good sign."

A look of relief flickered across Chuck's face as he whispered, "Thank you, God."

"What happened?" Alex managed to ask as the nurse continued on to the soldier who laid in the next cot.

"A bomb exploded near the tunnels where we were located. We were far enough away not to be seriously hurt, but shrapnel was everywhere. A large piece hit your leg."

It was then that Alex glanced down and saw the large, white bandage that encased his entire leg. He turned questioning eyes to Chuck as he continued.

"The doctor's didn't think they could save it, but we prayed, and God intervened."

"Then came the infection" Chuck shook his head.

"Fever ravaged your body, and when you didn't regain consciousness, the doctor's told us there was nothing more they could do. That was a week ago, yet today you are awake. Alex, God has spared your life."

Another week passed.

With every day, Alex's leg grew stronger, and the doctors grew more confident that, in time, he would regain full use of it. Until then, Alex would be sent home to recover.

While Alex was pleased at the thought of seeing Lydia once again, it pained him to think of the increasing number of men who were dying daily. Would victory ever be won? Daily, the nurses gathered around the small radio at the hospital and listened to the updates from the front. Another inch of ground gained. Another life lost. When would it end?

It was two days before Alex was set to leave.

Newly injured men had been filling up the hospital for the past few days as the battle raged on.

Among the latest sent in was Corporal Chuck MacIntosh.

Alex watched as they wheeled in his friend, and helped him onto the vacant cot next to Alex's bed. The soldier who had occupied it had died the night before. Yet another had paid the ultimate price for freedom.

When the nurses had left, Chuck told his story. He had been injured while rescuing a fallen soldier. He had managed to pull the injured man to safety, but a bullet had pierced his left shoulder.

Chuck grinned up at Alex with a pained
look in his eyes.

"So I figured I'd come and join you."
Alex smiled. Even in pain, Chuck was
always the optimist.

The evening passed quickly. Despite
the agonizing pain that Chuck was in, he
remained in good spirits.

Alex enjoyed this time he spent beside
his friend. The hours passed quickly as
they talked about what they would do
when they finally were able to go home.

"I want to become a preacher." Chuck
said. "With all that's gone on, this
world will need answers, and I intend to
show them The Way."

"First, you'll need a wife." Alex
laughed loudly.

Chuck grinned sheepishly, "You may be
right. Not too many churches out there
want a single preacher."

"The church would be lined up out the
door with all the single young women."
Alex teased.

Together they laughed until they hurt.
It felt good to seize a moment of
happiness amidst all the hurt.

Suddenly, Chuck's face sobered,
"Alex, will you promise me something?"

"Sure, buddy." Alex replied.

"If anything were to happen to me,
would you write my mother? I am all the
family she has left, and it would make

it easier if she were to know about it
from a friend."

"I will write her," Alex said, "But
you don't have anything to worry about.
Soon you'll be home."

"Thank you, my friend," Chuck
whispered. Slowly, his eyes closed, and
he drifted off into a peaceful sleep.

Moments later, Alex, too, joined him
in that land of slumber.

Alex was having a nightmare.

He was back on the front lines. He
could hear the loud roar of a plane as
it flew over head dropping bombs, and
leaving a path of deadly destruction in
it's wake. He could hear the screams of
the wounded men around him as the pain
tore through their bodies. And above all
he could hear the screaming cries of his
good friend, Corporal Chuck MacIntosh.

Alex woke up with a start.

An eerie orange glow lit up the
hospital. The heat was unbearable!
The screams he had heard in his
nightmare became a reality as he
realized that a bomb had fallen. And the
hospital was now on fire.

Chapter Four

The screams that had interrupted Alex's dreams had become a horrible, waking nightmare.

From the light of the flames that were greedily racing towards him, Alex could see the destruction left by the bomb that had been dropped mercilessly onto the unsuspecting hospital.

Portions of the roof had caved in, and debris was everywhere.

Alex hoisted himself off the bed, and looked for an escape route, but none seemed to present itself. Turning, he noticed a large beam, and a portion of the ceiling had fallen across the bed next to his.

"Chuck!" he gasped. The smoke stung his throat as he pushed the words past his parched lips.

Chuck's entire chest, and lower body lay crushed, and mangled beneath the cruel pile of debris. His screams had tapered off, and a low moan escaped his lips.

"Alex..."

Alex pushed himself forward, forgetting for a moment the unrelenting pain coursing through his leg, as well as his imminent danger. All he cared about was his friend.

He pushed, and pulled frantically at the beam that held his friend captive, but to no avail. Already, flames had begun to lick at the far end.

Chuck's arms reached towards Alex. Pain clouded his usually mischievous eyes, and a small red stain trickled out of the corner of Chuck's mouth as he pleaded.

"Remember..."

He raised his free arm, and grasped the dog tags that hung around his neck. With his last bit of remaining strength, he yanked them off, and deposited them into Alex's hand.

"Tell my mother...I'm with Jesus now..." his whisper was so faint that Alex could barely hear it over the roaring of the fire, and the screams of the doctor's, nurses, and patients as they stumbled blindly about looking for freedom.

"I promise, my friend" Alex stuffed the dog tags into his shirt pocket.

When he looked back at his friend, he realized that the brave courageous soldier had gone home. Not to his home in Toronto where his mother waited. No, Chuck had passed from this world to the next where there was neither pain, nor sorrow.

With a sad heart, Alex turned away.

Alex looked around frantically for a way out, but everywhere he looked, there was either debris, or flames.
Smoke stung his lungs, and eyes.
He ripped off his shirt, and covered his face.

Suddenly, a large section of the roof gave away. With the sudden burst of air,

the flames jumped even higher.
Unless, he found a way out soon, Alex
realized, it would be too late.

"Jesus," he cried out, "Guide my
steps!"

The fire burned hotter than ever now.
He could feel it's radiant heat, and he
wondered how much more he could endure.
He felt the hot metal of his dog tags as
they burned into his flesh. In his
frenzied state, Alex ripped off the
instigators of his added torture, and
flung them back towards the fire.

As he looked up, he thought for a
moment that he could see his friend
Chuck. Gone were the traces of pain.
Instead, his face was serene and
peaceful. And those mischievous eyes had
their sparkle back!

Chuck motioned him forward, and Alex
blindly followed. Looking up, Alex could
see the light as it broke forth out of
the eerie, orange night.

Morning had finally come.

With his last bit of strength slowly
waning, Alex pushed himself towards the
bright daylight as the image of Chuck
slowly faded.

Just as he reached it, a loud noise
tore through as the remaining roof, and
walls of the hospital collapsed.

But Alex was too close. He felt the
sickening thud as pieces from the roof
struck his head, and body, and he could
feel himself sinking slowly into
oblivion.

The shirt in his hands fell free, and

he could once again feel the heat of hot metal as it burned into his flesh.
His last thought as he faded into oblivion was that he couldn't wait until this was over so he could be with his one true love.

His head spinning, Alex managed to whisper
"Lydia"
Then the darkness overtook him

Chapter Five

It was November 11, 1918. People in the town danced, and shouted: "Victory for the Allied Forces!"

Lydia was glad the war was over, but afraid of the news that might reach her any day. It had been four months since she'd received the letter from Corporal Chuck MacIntosh.

That had been the last correspondence she had received.

Every day, she prayed-begging God to spare the life of the man she cherished with all her heart. Every day, the nagging suspicion that he had passed from this world to the next increased.

Despite the fact that her hope was fading, she remained firm in her belief that only God could intervene. It was in Him alone that she placed her trust.

It was a chilly day near the end of November when the dreaded news finally came.

Lydia was just finishing her morning lessons, when she heard the door of the little one-room school house creak open.

Looking up, she found herself staring at two men in uniform.

One man was mid-thirties, tall, with dark hair, and a serious look. The other was older, possibly mid-forties with graying hair, and a sadness in his eyes.

The medals that glistened against the stark contrast of their uniforms spoke of bravery, and valor.

From a glance one could tell that they were most comfortable in the thick of battle, weapons raised, fighting valiantly.

These were men of war.

But why had they come?

Their hats in their hands, they stepped forward as one.

"Ms. Lydia Thompson?"

Numbly, she nodded.

"We regretfully inform you that Corporal Alex Thorne was killed in action. We realize that you and Corporal Thorne were only engaged, however, he had listed you as his next of kin. He was a good man, and a valiant soldier who served our country well. Our condolences go out to you, ma'am."

Lydia felt the room begin to swirl

about her. Blackness threatened to overcome her. She reached out a hand to steady herself as she watched the eyes of her students turn from laughter to sadness.

These were good kids. They had joined her daily in her prayers for the troops, and especially for Alex's safety. Their faith had astounded her, and she, too, had joined them in their belief that Alex would return to them.
Where was God, and why, oh why, had he failed them?

She felt a steady hand against her arm as one of the uniformed soldiers asked, "Are you alright, ma'am?"

No, she was not all right. In fact, everything was wrong!

The war was over-had been for a few weeks. Alex should be coming home to her. They would be getting married! Raising a family! Growing old together!

Slowly, she willed herself to hear what the soldiers were saying

"Corporal Thorne was killed while hospitalized for an injury he received during active duty...He received a military burial near the place where he died...He was buried alongside other victims of the hospital bombing."

The men's voices droned on, but Lydia had heard enough. She felt as if her heart had died within her.

The realization had slowly dawned on her.

There would be no wedding.

In fact, there wouldn't even be a

funeral.

Her beloved Alex-the man she had loved with all her heart-was lying dead in a military grave overseas all alone. There would be no one by his graveside to mourn the man who once was. No one to place flowers in memorial to the life he once lived. There would be no great epitaph to tell of this man who lived, and was loved to the generations to come. No, there would only be a small white cross to forever mark the grave where he lay. A small white cross amongst thousands of others who had perished in the political insanity called war.

It pained Lydia to think that although Alex had fought valiantly on the battle front, he had not been able to defend himself or his countrymen from the cowardice that brought about their end as they lay recovering from the wounds inflicted from a cruel battlefield.

Agonizing grief overcame her, and a sob escaped her lips.

She fell heavily into the chair, and dropped her head onto her desk as a river of tears began to flow freely.

Never again would she see the face of her beloved, or be held in his strong, loving embrace. Never again would his warm lips brush softly against hers. Never again would she revel in how it felt to love and be loved.

She was destined to be alone. Destined never to marry the man of her dream, her heart's desire.

Destined to sit back while all that had been right, and good had been suddenly-painfully-torn from her in an instant.

This was her destiny.

Her fate, if you will.

God had forsaken her. Love had died, and, in its place bitterness began its reign.

Slowly, she stood to her feet. She willed her shaking legs to cease their trembling. She cleared her throat.

"Thank you, gentlemen, for informing me."

The calm, cold words seemed callous to her ears even as she spoke. But why should she care what people thought?

Her world had crumbled.

Alex was gone.

Chapter Six

It was a dark, moonlit night when Lydia reached Toronto.

Christmas vacation had come, and with it, Lydia had said her goodbye to both her students, and the small town where she had grown up.

Had it only been three short weeks since her world had crumbled?

The previous days had passed quickly as Lydia had thrown herself into her work. Her family had urged her to slow down, and take time to grieve, but Lydia had refused.

"I need to be strong for my students" she had insisted "They need me."

Deep down, Lydia knew she was only fooling herself.

She had pushed on, trying to forget the face of the man who haunted her dreams. The man she had loved was gone.

With Christmas approaching, Lydia had contacted her Uncle Herb, and Aunt Bertha in Toronto.

She had asked if they might like some company over the holidays. Knowing the situation that prompted her request, they had immediately sent word that they would be happy to have her company throughout the Christmas season.

Lydia felt a stab of fear as her train rolled into the station.

She was running.

Running from her self. Running from her past. And sadly enough, running from God.

Uncle Herb met her with a warm hug.

"Lydia, so good to see you again!"

Uncle Herb was a big man, somewhat overweight with a thick head of silver hair. He was her Dad's brother-the oldest of seven children-and Lydia's favorite uncle.

He helped her into the horse-drawn carriage, and with a quilt wrapped around her to ward off the winter chill, they set off down the streets of Toronto to the fancy Victorian house in the

suburbs that Uncle Herb and his wife,
Bertha called home.

Christmas had come and gone, but
Lydia's heavy heart remained.

She had run away, but the gnawing pain
had followed her.

She had been glad for the company of
her cousins, Liz, and Louie, over the
holidays.

Liz was now eighteen. She had married
last spring, and had moved into a lavish
home with her handsome husband, Michael
Worthington. Liz had married well, and
was very happy.

Louie had been a sergeant in the army
for the past two years. He was twenty-
one. Tall, blonde, and definitely the
ladies man. Someday, he would settle
down, but for now he was content basking
in the crowds of single women drawn to
him by his dashing good looks, crisp
uniform, and handsome smile.

Together, the four of them had
attended lavish parties, and balls
thrown over the Christmas season. They
had a great time.

But long after the sounds of the
laughter, and music had died, Lydia's
sadness remained. She had made the
effort to forget. She had tried to
laugh, and smile again. Tried to erase
the painful memories of a bygone day
when she had a bright future to

anticipate.

It was easier said than done.

Uncle Herb, and Aunt Bertha called Lydia into the study late one evening in early January.

Liz had gone back to her lavish home, and Louie had gone to visit a girl he had met while stationed in England.

The house was quiet, and Lydia could feel the loneliness overwhelm her once again as she stepped into the study where her Aunt and Uncle waited.

"Lydia, we have a proposition to make" Uncle Herb began.

That was her uncle, always straight to the point. Lydia smiled, and waited for him to continue.

"We would like you to stay here with us for a few months. The house is much too lonely now that our own children are gone."

"Thank you, Uncle Herb, and Aunt Bertha, but I don't think..."

Uncle Herb held up his hand to stop her before she could decline. "We also have a condition." He motioned to his wife, Bertha.

"I have recently spoken to a friend of mine who volunteers at a convalescent hospital right her in Toronto." Bertha said in her soft, lilting voice.

"She, too, suffered a great loss during the war, but she has found a purpose once again helping the wounded soldiers find hope."

"But I don't think I could..."Lydia began to protest, but her Uncle Herb cut her off again.

"Lydia, you would be doing your country a great service. And what better way to remember Alex than to help the soldiers who fought alongside him as they recover from their injuries?"

Lydia had to admit they had a point. Besides, if the situation was reversed, and Alex lay wounded in some convalescent hospital, wouldn't she want him to have the best care?

"I will look into it" she said somewhat reluctantly.

Sunny Brook Convalescent Care Center was located on ten acres of beautifully landscaped ground that bordered on a small, peaceful lake. A bubbling brook ran throughout the property, and the park-like setting gave it a very peaceful atmosphere.

The building itself was a tall, white mansion that had been converted into a care facility. Huge white pillars supported the gabled roof, and a large veranda wrapped around the side.

Lydia stepped out of the carriage. Stopping in the midst of the drive to admire the scenery, she gazed at the serene beauty all around her.

Sunny Brook Convalescent Care Center seemed more like a peaceful, vacation get-away than a home for the sick, and infirmed!

This place was beautiful!

She turned quickly at the sound of rapidly approaching hooves. A horse galloped up the drive, the carriage behind it bouncing mercilessly. It only took one look to show that the poor beast had been spooked, and was now careening at a full gallop fully unconscious of the driver who was trying , unsuccessfully, to regain control.

It was too little too late!

Lydia didn't have time to move out of the way as horse, and carriage slammed into her body.

She felt the sickening thud. Felt as the wind was knocked from her lungs. She felt herself flying high through the air. And pain.

Intense pain.

That was the last thing she remembered.

Chapter Seven

The rolling motion of the ship was enough to make anyone sick. Added to that was the cries of the wounded soldiers that lay in the close quarters below deck, their suffering maximized by the thrashing waves the ship had just encountered.

But in spite of their pain, hope lit their faces, and anticipation shimmered in their sad eyes.

They were finally going home.

Some were mere boys. They had joined full of heroic dreams, and the foolishness common to the young. Anxious to be part of the action, their youth had been unwittingly snatched from them by the cruel, hard war. The twinkle was gone from their eyes, the gaiety from their laugh.

They had fought hard, and succeeded, but at what cost?

Still others were grown men. They had left their wives, children, and homes. They had given up all that was dear to them. Only to be returned maimed, injured in body and spirit-a shadow of their former selves.

Why, oh, why, had the war come?

In the farthest corner of the ship, lay a soldier staring vacantly into the darkness of the shadows. Some would say that he was young, but the pain, and sadness about him made him look like an old man.

One thing was certain, the war had been very cruel to this young corporal.

Large bandages encircled both his legs. Another was wrapped tightly around his head. His hands bore the small scars left by the extreme heat he had endured.

Thick tufts of dark hair could be seen peeking through the top of his bright, white head bandages, and his finely cut features peering through rough stubble gave witness to the fact that this soldier had once been a very handsome, young man.

But it was his eyes that bore the most sadness.

The dark, brown eyes that would have once held girls spellbound, now gazed about vacantly.

This soldier had wished for the painful memories of war to go away.

His wish had been granted.

A short, stout nurse with red hair, and a bubbly English accent, leaned over the soldier in the farthest bed. She adjusted his blankets, and pillow.

"Are you comfortable, corporal?" she questioned.

The corporal nodded.

Yes, with all the pain medication he had been given, and the doctor's, and nurses good care, he was comfortable. But the pain in his body did not compare to the pain and sadness he felt inside.

Who was he?

Was he once a man whom people liked, or was he hated, and despised? Was he a man who did good deeds, or was he selfish, and unforgiving? Was he a Christian man with a firm belief in God, or was he a man without faith or hope?

His finger's grasped the small dog tags that hung around his neck. The spot where they had burned his flesh had almost healed. Absently, he turned them around, and gazed at the small inscription on them.

For the hundredth time since the fateful day when the world he had known ended, and this new one had started afresh, he wondered about the life he had left behind.

Did he have a family? Was there someone out there who loved him?

He reached for the small Bible the nurse had given him. She had hoped he would find the peace he needed. Instead, he found himself haunted with the unknown.

The nurse patted his arm re-assuring him that everything would be all right once he reached home.

He wasn't so sure.

And where was home? Did he live in a lavish, modern house, or a small farm on the outskirts of town?

He would soon find out.

The ship was due to dock any day now, and he would embark on his new life.

After he finished recovering.

The nurse had finished changing his bandages now, and she stood back, and smiled at him.

"Amnesia is a hard thing, but I am praying for you"

She patted the small Bible she had given him.

"Let me know if you need anything at all, Corporal Chuck MacIntosh" she said in her bubbly voice as she turned away.

And with that she was gone.

Chapter Eight

Lydia moaned as she tried to open her eyes. Her head throbbed. Her body ached.

She could hear concerned voices echoing around her.

"Is she all right?" A familiar male voice asked no one in particular "Lydia, can you hear me?"

Lydia moaned again as she recognized the deep voice of her Uncle Herb.

"I'm sorry...so sorry...The horse was spooked"

This voice seemed to be coming from another male.

Lydia tried again to open her eyes, but the pain made it impossible. Flashes of light seemed to dance around her eyes, but she could not make out any shapes. Blood trickled from a large gash above her eye, and her head throbbed mercilessly.

"I can't see!" She cried out in terror. She tried to sit up, and felt a strong arm encircle her shoulders.

"Take it easy, Lydia" Uncle Herb said

to her "You had a very nasty accident. We're going to take you inside so that a doctor can have a good look at you." And with that he scooped her up into his strong arms, and carried her through the front doors of Sunny Brook Care Center.

The smell of disinfectant greeted Lydia as she was carried into the convalescent hospital. While the outside looked like a dreamy paradise, the interior definitely met the high hospital standards.

A doctor checked her over, his voice optimistic.

"There is no sign of broken bones" He was saying "However, she did bruise her ribs quite badly, and she has a bad concussion. Considering the severity of her accident, she is a very lucky girl."

"What about my sight?" Lydia asked, fearing the answer she might hear, yet knowing she must ask.

"I am sorry, ma'am" The doctor said softly "With the kind of head trauma you received, it is much too early to tell" He paused a second before he continued.

"Hopefully, in time, you will see again. Until then...all we can do is hope..."

"...And pray..."Uncle Herb added.

As the doctor prepared to stitch up the gash, Uncle Herb took his leave. He promised to return in the morning with

Aunt Bertha, and with that he was gone.

After stitching up the gash above her eye, the doctor began wrapping bandages around Lydia's head. She clenched her teeth as the rough, white material brushed against the freshly closed sutures.

"You can stay here tonight in one of the empty rooms" A nurse with a strong, English accent told her." Tomorrow, we will arrange for you to be moved to a more suitable facility."

Two nurses hoisted her onto a small cot. The wheels on the cot clanged loudly as they pushed her down a long corridor, and into a bright room.

"I will be back to check on you." The nurse with the bubbly accent told her as she fluffed Lydia's pillows, and covered her with a fresh, wool blanket.   "If there's anything at all you need, just let me know." And then they were gone, and Lydia was left all alone with her thoughts.

Was she going to remain blind? Would she ever see again?

With these thoughts came the images of her accident. The driver screaming. The horses bolting with that frightened look in their eyes. The crash of the horses, and carriage as it slammed into her fragile body. The sensation of flying through the air.

She thrashed around and cried out.

Suddenly a comforting voice floated through the walls, it's timbers echoing down the lonely corridors of the convalescent hospital.

Somewhere nearby, someone was reading the scriptures aloud.

Lydia recognized the passage from Psalms chapter 46:

"God is our refuge and strength, a very present help in trouble...Therefore will not we fear...The Lord of hosts is with us..."

The words slowly soothed the pain Lydia was feeling both physically, and spiritually. The realization suddenly dawned on her that God was still in control.

He hadn't gone anywhere.

While the world had seemingly spun out of control with madness, God had still reigned supreme.

When Alex had died in that horrible accident, and her world had shattered, God had been there to pick up the pieces. Even in the midst of her own accident, God had been there, and had spared her life.

Tears trickled, unbidden, down her face as the nurse returned to check on her.

"I heard you cry out, dear." She said in a soothing voice as if she were comforting a small child." Are you all right?"

Lydia nodded. "That scripture was beautiful. It made me realize that even with all that has gone on in the world, God is still here, comforting us, and giving us hope."

"You must have heard Corporal

MacIntosh." The nurse said as she patted Lydia's hand reassuringly." He, too, is learning that God is still in control. The corporal suffered greatly both physically, and spiritually while on the battle field, but God has been there for him through it all. Since he has arrived home, that passage has become very dear to him. He has started reading it aloud every evening to the other soldiers, and they have found comfort in it as well."

"Will you thank him for reading the scriptures aloud?" Lydia asked the nurse.

"Oh course, honey." The nurse replied as she left the room to resume her rounds.

Lydia closed her eyes. A deep peace had settled over her. She could still hear Corporal MacIntosh as he continued reading to the other soldiers on his ward.

As she drifted off to sleep, the voice seemed to take on a familiar tone.

Memories that she had tried so hard to bury were suddenly resurrected.

Sleep threatened to overcome her, but she pushed against it, willing herself to remember where she had heard that voice before. In an instant it came to her.

"Alex." She whispered.

Before she could fathom whether or not she was awake or dreaming, the powerful, healing sleep had overcome her.

With a smile on her lips, Lydia had drifted off into the peaceful land of slumber.

Chapter Nine

Just two doors down the hall from
Lydia, a soldier opened his eyes to the
smiling red-haired nurse with the bubbly
English accent. Her name was Carolyn
Johnson, and she seemed to bring
sunshine wherever she went.

The corporal smiled as she bustled
around his room, settling his breakfast
tray on a nearby table, and pulling open
the curtains.

"Good Morning, Corporal MacIntosh!"
She gushed "Just look at the lovely day
out there today!"

She waved a hand towards the window
she had just propped open.

A small chickadee fluttered by, and
chirped a pretty melody. The sunlight
danced around his room, and a cool
breeze caressed his face-a very cool
breeze!

"Hey!" Chuck said with a grin, "Close
that window before I catch my death from
pneumonia!" He flung a pillow good-
naturedly at the nurse who ducked and
then threw it back at him.

Nurse Johnson laughed as she closed
the window tightly, "Just thought you
might be interested in what is going on
with the rest of the world."

Chuck's face instantly sobered.

What was going on in the world? There was so much more than what he had become accustomed to here at Sunny Brook Care Center.

He wondered what life would be like once he had recovered enough to leave. And where would he go?

He had expected someone to meet him upon his arrival. Someone-anyone-to come, and greet him by name. Someone to fill him in on the life he once had before the terrible loss of his memory.

He had hoped, and waited, but to no avail.

No one had come.

In fact, in the past few weeks that he'd been home he hadn't had a single visitor!

Who was the real Chuck MacIntosh? Was he alone in this world?

"A young girl was injured here yesterday," Nurse Carolyn said as she changed the bandages on Chuck's injured legs," She was admitted overnight, and today they will be moving her to a hospital in the city." She shook her head, "The poor thing lost her sight."

Chuck's heart went out to the poor, young girl who had been injured.

"She heard you reading Psalms 46 last evening. " the nurse continued, "She asked me to thank you as it brought her much comfort."

"That verse has been a comfort to me as well," said Chuck.

Unselfish to a fault, he wished he could do something to ease the suffering of the poor girl down the hall. A thought flickered into his mind. While he might not be able to do anything physically to help her, he could most certainly pray for her.

"What's the young girl's name?" he questioned.

"Lydia Thompson" said the nurse.

Chuck felt as if a light had been turned on in his head, and for the first time since the horrible fire, Chuck had a brief memory.

He saw snow softly falling, and heard the joyful sound of sleigh bells.

He could hear the faint strains of a Christmas Carol.

It was all so magical!

And Chuck was not alone. A beautiful, young woman sat next to him, her face aglow she gazed out at the wonder of it all.

Love.

It hammered in his chest so strongly, Chuck thought he might burst.

Then, just as suddenly as the memory had come, it faded away once again out of his grasp leaving behind a gaping, loneliness in it's place.

Chuck turned to Nurse Carolyn Johnson.

"Do you think I might be able to see her before she leaves?"

"I would like to pray with her" he added

Nurse Carolyn smiled, "I think we can arrange that" she said as she bustled out the door.

"Lydia is expecting you"
Nurse Carolyn said as she bustled back
into Chuck's room a few moments later
with another nurse, and a small
wheelchair.

Together, they lifted Chuck's tall,
muscular frame into the chair, and
wheeled him out into the hall.

They stopped two doors down, and
pushed Chuck's wheelchair through the
narrow doorway.

Chuck gasped.

A young woman lay on the bed, her
identity unrecognizable. Her face was
red, and swollen, and a fresh, white
bandage covered her forehead, and eyes.
She lay propped against the pillows, her
pale arms in stark contrast to the dark
green of the linens in spite of the
ugly, dark bruises that seemed to
encompass them.

She looked so small, and helpless,
that Chuck wanted to take her in his
arms, and will her to mend.

Instead, he willed himself to speak,

"Lydia," he said. His voice had taken
on a strange, husky quality as his
confidence began to waver. "I heard
about your accident, and I was wondering
if you would mind if I said a prayer for
you."

"Not at all," Lydia's voice sounded

small, and weak. "Please…Pray."

Chuck's voice rose in supplication to his Maker, "God, we pray this day that you will be with Lydia. Touch her with your healing, cleansing power...Amen"

As he finished, a peace seemed to flood the small, hospital room.

Chuck turned to the nurse, and nodded.

As she wheeled him towards the open door, he glanced back at the poor, young creature who had suffered so much.

He wished he could make all her pain and suffering go away.

A sudden urge of protectiveness overwhelmed him.

"I will continue to pray, Lydia," he whispered, and with that, the nurse wheeled him out into the corridor, and out of Lydia's life forever.

Chapter Ten

"Flowers for you, Miss"

Lydia lifted her head at the sound of the hesitant male voice.

"Thank you" she said softly.

Two days had now passed since her dreadful accident. She had been moved from the convalescent care home to another hospital in the city the previous day.

Her wounds, and bruises ached horribly, and her sight had still not returned.

Footsteps approached Lydia's bedside, and she heard the small clunk as a vase of flowers were deposited on her bedside table.

"I just wanted to come by, and say how sorry I am," the youthful voice went on uncertainly, "If I had just controlled the horse better, this would never of happened."

"You were driving the carriage?" Lydia managed to ask feebly.

"Yes, Miss," Lydia heard feet shuffle nervously, "My name is Mickey O'Dell, and I'm terribly sorry. If there is anything I can do..."His voice trailed off.

Lydia sighed, "Accidents happen, Mickey. I'm sure that you did your best to control the horse."

"But I feel responsible. How can I ever make this up to you, Miss?" Mickey lamented.

"Lydia."

"Pardon, Miss?"

"My name is Lydia, not 'miss', and you can start by sitting down, and talking to me," Lydia's weak voice began to gather strength as she continued in her best schoolteacher's voice, "Laying here with nothing to do is driving me mad, so why don't you begin by telling me about yourself."

In her time as a teacher, Lydia had learned the best way to handle an upset child was to first distract them, then deal with the underlying issues once the child had opened up to her. It was this tactic she now applied to the unwitting Mickey O'Dell.

The sound of a chair scraping against the rough floor met Lydia's ears, and then Mickey's voice began.

"As I said, my name is Mickey O'Dell, and I was born here in Toronto. I was orphaned at the age of fourteen, and spent my days on the streets.

I looked for work anywhere I could, but work was hard to find. A kind lady, and her son met me on the streets one day. They helped me find God, and get on my feet. I got a good job working as a courier, and volunteered for the Army at the start of the war.

We saw some action in France, and I was sent home with the rest of the Troops at the end of the War. I sought out my old boss, and he gave me my old job back.

I now have a small apartment on the outskirts of the city where I live with my best friend, an old dog I rescued named Scrap."

"Interesting name for a dog," Lydia mused.

"Found him at an old metal yard," Mickey laughed as his confidence grew, "He was a shaggy little guy, and half-starved, too, but he came around. He's the only real family I have."

Lydia managed a shaky smile.

"Do you like dogs?" Mickey asked her for lack of a better route in which to steer this rather awkward conversation.

"I love all animals, but horses are off my list-at least for a little while," she laughed softly, and was surprised when Mickey joined in.

"Lydia," he whispered gently, "I have truly enjoyed our conversation. You have such a great attitude about you even in spite of the...accident..."his voice trailed off.

Lydia suddenly felt drawn to the young man by her side.

Maybe it was the fact that she was glad to have someone to talk to, but suddenly she found herself opening up to Mickey. The young man had sincerity about him that many lacked, and Lydia was glad for the diversion from her current state.

In spite of the fact that they had just met, Lydia had soon found herself recounting to Mickey the heartbreaking details of how she had come to live in Toronto with her Aunt and Uncle. As she told him of Alex's grim death overseas, her eyes once again produced a torrential river of tears that coursed past the bandages, and over her face.

"There, there now," Mickey soothed her as he softly brushed her tear-stained face with his clean, crisp handkerchief, "Please, don't cry," he whispered.

He reached for her hand, and she marvelled at the strength which he possessed as he leaned forward, and clasped her hand tightly to his chest. She found herself clinging to his hand as though it were a lifeline.

"The war is over. The turmoil in your life is past. God is here with you, and He will help you begin anew." His deep voice reassured, and calmed her.

In this time in her life she realized that Mickey was just what she had needed.

God had sent this kind Christian man to her under the worst possible circumstances, but maybe it was in His Plan all along.

It was just like God to stop her dead in her self-loathing tracks, and turn things around for the better.

Almost two hours had passed before Mickey rose to leave.

"I am afraid I must go," he said regretfully, "But I promise you I will continue to pray for your complete healing."

Lydia knew he meant both physical, and spiritual healing, and she was grateful for his prayers.

"Thank you, Mickey" she said as he turned to leave.

"May I come visit you again? "he asked suddenly as he stopped hesitantly by the door.

"I would love to have you come by," she replied. And, surprisingly enough, Lydia found she truly meant it.

Was God finally closing the chapter on her previous life with Alex, and opening a new with Mickey?

Or did his Plan have yet another purpose?

"Until then..."Mickey said gallantly.

And with that he was gone....

Chapter Eleven

Mickey woke up the next morning with one thought on his mind.

Lydia.

In spite of the dire circumstances in which they met, Mickey couldn't help but feel that God had brought her into his life for a reason.

His thoughts drifted back to the previous day.

Lydia had every reason to blame him for the accident, but, instead, she chose to forgive and forget. Even more unbelievable-she had even gone, and offered her friendship to him, confided in him, and invited him back.

"What a girl," Mickey said to himself as he ran a comb through his unruly brown hair, and prepared for another day of work.

Reaching down, he gave Scrap a quick pat on the head.

"Have a good day, old boy," he said fondly to the large, scruffy-looking dog.

Scrap wagged his tail happily.

Grabbing his coat, and hat, Mickey left for another day of work for the courier service.

"Good Morning, Corporal. Today is a good day," the cheery voice was punctuated by the sound of the curtains being drawn open, and bright light streaming into the drab room.

Chuck opened his eyes, and groaned at the sight of the bubbly nurse, Carolyn Johnson.

"Today is the day you go home!"

Home.

The word should have brought him comfort, yet it seemed somehow cold and unfriendly. What would home be like?

For the three months since he had arrived at Sunny Brook Convalescent Care Center, Chuck had labored hard to recover from his injuries.

He had pushed himself hard to regain the full use of his injured legs, and his efforts had been rewarded. Although he still walked with a cane, the doctors were hopeful that the slight limp that still remained would soon disappear, and Chuck would be as good as new.

But, in spite of the therapy the doctors had prescribed, Chuck knew he would never be 'as good as new' again.

He forced a smile at his cheery nurse.

"Yes, Nurse Johnson, today is the day!"

Mickey smiled to himself as he finished up his daily deliveries. He knew deep down that his good spirits were due to none other than the lovely Lydia Thompson.

For the past few weeks, he had spent every spare minute with the charming, young lady.

She was a bright ray of sunshine in his otherwise mundane existence, and he loved how she made him feel when he was with her.

Lydia's injuries had slowly begun to heal, but, as yet, her sight had not returned.

Daily, the doctors examined her eyes, hopeful that her sight was regained. Daily they had hoped for the best-and faced the worst.

Lydia's aunt and uncle had paid for the best eye doctors that money could buy, but all they could do in the end was hope-and pray.

His last parcel delivered, Mickey looked at his pocket watch, and was pleased to see that he was finished early.

As he did a few times each week, Mickey turned his carriage towards the home of his good friend, and mentor, Julia MacIntosh.

Julia McIntosh untied her apron, and

slung it over the back of a ladder-backed chair.

Wisps of graying hair had somehow escaped the small bun at the nape of her neck, and she reached up and tucked them behind her ear.   Grabbing a handkerchief, she dabbed it in cool water, and touched it to her forehead before sitting tiredly in her favorite chair.

Six dozen or so chocolate chip cookies lay cooling evidence of the afternoon's labors.

Tears glistened in Julia's eyes as she recalled bygone days.

Chocolate chip had been her son's favorite.

Today she made them in his memory.

Her mind drifted to the day when the horrible news had reached her that her son was MIA and presumed dead. She had tried to be hopeful when deep down she knew that her dear boy would not be coming home.

Julia, like thousands of other mothers, had been forced to sacrifice her only son for the sake of freedom.

His memory was everywhere-especially in the work they had started together helping the poor in their city. Lives had been changed, and hearts had been turned toward their Maker.

As much as Julia was saddened at her loss, she was glad that she knew her dear boy was with his Savior whom he loved so much.

She had started to nod off when she

heard the front door open.

Leaping to her feet in a panic, she stared in horror at the tall, dark hair of the man who stood hesitantly before her.

Still half asleep, she noticed only one thing.

The big stick the man carried.

Petrified, and sure that the towering young man with the weary-looking eyes surely meant her harm, she screamed at the top of her lungs.

Chapter Twelve

For days Corporal Chuck MacIntosh had anticipated his homecoming with a mixture of fear, and excitement.

'What will 'home' really be like?' he had wondered only moments earlier as he lightly tapped on the front door of the modest, white house in the Toronto suburbs that the Army had told him was his home.

Standing here now, he was sure even his worst nightmare couldn't compare.

There had been no answer to his knock, but the door had been slightly ajar. Chuck had opened it hesitantly, unsure of what might lay inside.

"Hello?" he had called as the big wooden door had creaked open, "Is anybody home?"

Silence had greeted him.

"Hello?" he called again as he slowly made his way with the help of his cane into the large, country kitchen.

He breathed deeply as the sweet aroma of freshly baked chocolate chip cookies assaulted his sense of smell, and he felt a small glimmer of hope flicker inside him.

Perhaps he did have a family. Perhaps they had heard of his extensive injuries, and had wanted him to heal completely before they were reunited. Perhaps, in spite of his memory loss, Chuck was finally going to have the homecoming he so longed for.

Suddenly a scream rent through the air interrupting his thoughts.

In front of him stood the middle-aged woman from his photograph.

"Mother? Is that you?" he whispered recalling the sweet, loving message that she had penned to her dear son.

All the anticipation he had felt suddenly turned to dread.

That sweet, little woman now faced him with a look of sheer terror on her face as she screamed at the top of her lungs.

'Was she mad?' Chuck wondered incredulously,' Had the war been too much for this poor soul?

How could he possibly allay this petrified woman's fears?

Suddenly, he remembered the photograph. Chuck lifted his hand to retrieve it from his coat pocket, but before he could, he was tackled from behind.

He felt himself falling, and with a sickening thud his head hit the edge of the kitchen table.

The photograph in his pocket fluttered to the floor as the world around Chuck swirled into black.

Mickey was relieved he had come to visit Julia when he did. Otherwise, he would never have seen the tall intruder who had entered, uninvited, into her peaceful home.

He had just pulled up when he saw her door ajar, and heard her ear-piercing screams. Throwing caution to the wind, he had bounded up the front steps and into Julia's cozy home.

At the sight of the tall, dark-haired man standing so foreboding in front of Julia, Mickey had felt the blood rush through his veins.

Julia MacIntosh had been through so much this past year. Her only son had perished on the battlefield-a casualty of the cruel war that had ravaged the world.

A wave of sadness encompassed Mickey as he thought of Julia's son. Four years older, Chuck had been like an older brother to Mickey throughout his teenage years.

Together Julia, and her son had helped Mickey find a new lease on life when he found himself alone, and living on the streets at the age of fourteen.

It was under Julia's instruction that Mickey had come to learn, and trust solely in his Creator. Julia had even used her influence to help him get his job at the courier.

Yes, Julia MacIntosh was a wonderful, Godly woman, and Mickey loved her as if she were his own Mother.

Another scream rent the air and the tall, foreboding man with the cane quickly reached up his hand.

Fearing he was about to strike the poor, helpless Julia MacIntosh, Mickey did the only thing he could think of. Using all of his strength, Mickey hurled himself into the intruder, and tackled him.

With a terrible thud the man's head hit the kitchen table, and he fell heavily to the floor.

Mickey rolled the man over, and was relieved to see he was unconscious, but still alive. Intruder, or not, Mickey would never wish anyone dead.

Suddenly, a small gasp escaped the lips of Julia MacIntosh as she stooped over, and picked up a tattered photograph that had fluttered to the floor. Shock registered across her face as she shakily lifted the photograph and examined it.

Mickey looked in surprise as he realized it was a photograph of Julia.

"This was the photograph I sent to my dear Charles," Julia finally managed as the emotion ran thick through her voice.

Her eyes drifted to the unconscious man who lay on her kitchen floor.

She sprang into action at the sight of the large knot that was beginning to form on his head.

"Help me lay him on the bed in the guest room," she ordered Mickey, "And then send for the doctor at once!"

"But what if he wakes up?" Mickey started to protest, but Julia quickly silenced him.

"This man must have known my Charles. That makes him family." she said emphatically.

Mickey must have known it was useless to argue, as he turned to the man who now lay prone on the kitchen floor.

Grappling under the dead weight of the tall stranger, Julia, and Mickey managed to carry him into the guest quarters, and hefted him up on the bed.

A low moan escaped the man's lips as Mickey hurried to the door to retrieve the nearest physician.

Julia sponged the growing lump on the poor man's head as the questions began to swirl in her head.

Just who was this tall intruder? Was he truly a friend of Charles? Or was he another in a long line of men who tried to take advantage of a poor widow who was only now suffering the loss of her only child?

One thing seemed strange.

If he was a friend, then why in the world had he called her 'Mother'?

Chapter Thirteen

Lydia trembled as she sat in the office of Dr. Jefferson Montgomery. Today was the day when the doctors would finally remove the last of the awful bandages. Today was the day when Lydia would know whether or not her sight would ever be regained.

The doctor's cheery attitude did nothing to alleviate her fears, and she found herself sending a whispered prayer towards heaven.

Dr. Montgomery began the slow process of removing the bandages that covered her damaged eyes, and Lydia felt an involuntary shudder ripple through her very being.

What if she never regained her sight? How would she ever be able to cope with the loss of yet another vital part of her when she was still so vulnerable?

"Dear God", she found herself murmuring, "I know deep down that no matter what You have a Plan, and a Purpose for my life. I only ask God that you will be with me now. Guide and strengthen me-no matter what the outcome may be!"

Lydia hadn't even realized she'd said her prayer aloud until she felt Aunt Bertha squeeze her hand, and whisper a soft, "Amen." How grateful Lydia was to have her aunt's gentle support at a time like this!

Finally, the doctor had removed the last bandage. "Take your time, Lydia," Doctor Montgomery said, "Allow your eyes to slowly adjust to your surroundings. Now tell me...do you see anything?"

Lydia felt fresh tears burn her useless eyes as she shook her head.

"Just give it some time," the good doctor said reassuringly as he handed her a handkerchief to dry her tears.

For a brief second, Lydia could almost make out the small figure of Doctor Montgomery. She gasped, and looked again.

Yes, she was definitely seeing something!

She was about to shout for joy when a loud commotion at the door caused her to turn. She shifted her focus to an anxious young man bursting excitedly through the door.

"Come quick! There's a man at the MacIntosh place, and he's hurt pretty bad!"

The young man's eyes briefly took in the room until at last they locked on Lydia's. His face registered shock, but only for a brief moment for Lydia was staring at the man as if she were seeing a ghost.

Images flooded back to her of another young man. His hair, too, had been black, and his eyes had sparkled with love for her alone. Oh, how she missed that man!

"Lydia?" the young man whispered as he approached her, "Lydia? Can you see me?"

Mickey had hoped, and prayed for this moment. He had grown so fond of Lydia, yet he knew she would never be more than a mere friend unless she could see again.

Although Mickey knew that Lydia had forgiven him for the accident, he knew he would never be able to forgive himself for the pain he had caused if she was blinded for life.

Hope turned to joy as the dark-haired beauty nodded.

For a brief second, Mickey considered taking her in his arms, and kissing her.

Nothing would stand in his way now! He stepped forward, but Lydia's incredulous words stopped him dead in his tracks.

"Yes, Alex...I see you!"

Lydia had instantly recognized Mickey the moment she saw him.

Images of those last few moments before her accident had been permanently seared into her mind. Mickey's handsome face, etched with concern, had been the very last face she had seen before her sight had been stolen from her.

Even though she had hoped and prayed for the return of her sight, she had not been prepared for the emotions that overwhelmed her.

It had been Mickey's dark, black hair, and dancing eyes that had catapulted her back to another time, and another man-her Alex!

Through shimmering eyes she had nodded, and when she was finally able, it was Alex to whom she spoke.

Her heart ached as she heard her voice echo the name of her one true love, and a sob escaped from her throat.

Alex was gone, and all that was left was to pick up the pieces, and try to go on.

She looked at the crest-fallen face of Mickey O'Dell, and Lydia hoped her friendship had not led him on.

Here was a kind, young man-that she could tell just by looking at him. Unfortunate circumstances had caused their paths to cross, yet Lydia knew deep down that it must be a part of God's Plan.

Mickey was a gentle, handsome young man. He was good, kind, and, best of all, a devoted Christian.

Yes, Mickey was perfect in all ways-except one.

Mickey was not-nor ever could be-her Alex....

Chapter Fourteen

Mickey rushed to Lydia's side feeling his hopes and dreams shatter into a million pieces.

Looking into her eyes, he slowly realized that no matter how he felt about Lydia, she could never fully be his.

Her Alex was her world, and dead or living, he could never take Alex's place.

He gathered her in his arms, and held her close as the emotion threatening to overwhelm him.

This was the girl who had become his dearest friend. Some would say they had met by chance, but Mickey believed God had a plan in place in spite of the tragedy surrounding their initial encounter.

Even in her infirmity, she had brought light and gladness to his soul. She was like a breath of fresh air on a warm summer day...a ray of sunshine peeking through the dark clouds after a long storm...

Lydia could never be his for Lydia had only ever had one true love.

His name was Alex, and he lay silent in a shallow grave in a far away land with a small white cross to mark the spot where he would forever sleep.

Selflessly, Mickey vowed in his heart to be there for Lydia no matter what.

He would look after her, and love her as if she were his own sister. Slowly, he released her from his crushing embrace.

"Lydia", he whispered as tears coursed unbidden over his bewhiskered face, and a smile of sincere happiness spread across his lips

"I am so very happy for you!"

Lydia gazed in wonder at her surroundings.

She felt as if she were viewing the world for the very first time. The light, shapes, and colors threatened to overwhelm her.

Aunt Bertha leaned over her. Her eyes misty with the emotion of the miracle she had just witnessed.

"Thank you God!" she whispered as she gave her niece a warm embrace.

Mickey pulled himself away to help the doctor gather up his bag, and the supplies he would need to help the man who lay injured at the MacIntosh home. As he hurried out to his horse, and carriage, he heard a small voice cry out.

"Wait!"

Turning, he realized Lydia was cautiously approaching the carriage.

"Please...this is a day for

miracles...Let me come too!"

Mickey opened his mouth to protest, but Doctor Montgomery cut him off.

"Why not, Lydia? I could always use a good nurse! Just be careful not to overdo it!" he cautioned with a smile.

"I won't!" Lydia promised as she slid into the small carriage next to the good doctor, and they started off toward the MacIntosh home.

Chapter Fifteen

Corporal Chuck MacIntosh moaned as he slowly regained consciousness.

A doctor with a full head of silver hair was bandaging up the wound on his throbbing head as another man leaned over eyeing him suspiciously.

"Who are you?"

Chuck moaned again as he was again assaulted by another bout of pain. He wished the room would stop spinning so he could get a better look at the young man who peered down at him so suspiciously.

He could hear two women talking quietly to each other as they bustled about.

Was one of them his mother?

The pain was unbearable as he strained to focus. The light streaming through the window seemed to burn his eyes. He raked his fingers through his thick black hair, and felt a stab of pain as his fingers came into contact with the crisp white bandage that covered the gash on his forehead.

"Leave that be, son" Doctor Montgomery cautioned "You have an awful gash on that head, and probably a concussion as well. It will take some time for you to heal from this, but from the looks of you, you have been through much worse!"

"Yes, sir" Chuck said obediently.

He silently wished they would all just leave him alone so he could close his eyes and drift off into peaceful slumber.

The doctor stood to take his leave, and a small woman with graying hair accompanied him to the door. Chuck wondered who the woman could be.

Was she his mother?

His eyes shifted back to the young man who was looking at him so suspiciously. He remembered the stranger's earlier query, and struggled to answer it.

"I... am...Corporal...Chuck...MacIntosh" he managed faintly.

All at once the man sprang to his feet. Anger shone in his dark eyes, and when he spoke it was with an air of protectiveness.

"I knew Corporal Chuck MacIntosh, he was like a brother to me! You, sir, are not him!

Corporal MacIntosh is dead!"

The room swam around Chuck as this new

information swirled in his foggy brain.
He struggled to grasp hold of reality,
but the pain overtook him.

He heard a gasp, followed by a loud
crash, and a woman crying out, but he
could not fathom what she said.

Slowly, the black tunnel swirled
around him, and he drifted once again
into the land of the unconscious.

Lydia watched as the doctor hovered
over the injured man.

She recalled the story of his
intrusion into Julia MacIntosh's home,
and wondered for the fifteenth time
exactly who he was.

Was he some evil stranger out to do
the poor widow harm? There were so many
unscrupulous souls out there today
anxious to take advantage of the kindest
of hearts.

Doctor Montgomery hadn't needed her
assistance after all, but she had
lingered with Julia in the doorway just
in case her services were required.
Julia's serene personality reminded
Lydia of her own mother, and a stab of
homesickness surged through her for the
first time since she had arrived.

It was quickly dissipated. Without her
Alex, it was not home.

The doctor had finished and Julia had
escorted him to the door.

Mickey stood glaring down at the

stranger, and Lydia smiled. Mickey was such a good and gentle soul, but he was so very protective of the people he cared about!

Suddenly, the stranger spoke, and Lydia heard his weak voice state his name

"I...am...Corporal...Chuck...MacIntosh..."

She stood transfixed with the wash basin she had brought in clenched with trembling hands. Time seemed to stand still as a gasp escaped her.

She never heard Mickey's harsh reply for her mind had recognized a certain timber in the voice of the weak stranger.

The world for her ceased to exist as the name, "Alex" was wrenched from her paralyzed lips.

Emotions she had fought to suppress flooded her entire being. She barely heard the clatter as the ceramic basin slipped from her grasp and shattered into a million pieces. Instead, she flung herself across the room and fell to her knees.

"Alex?" she whispered incredulously "Alex!"

But the man on the bed had slipped back into a coma.

Chapter Sixteen

The dark-haired girl leaned over him as his eyelids slowly fluttered open. Her hair lay frazzled around her face, but love glistened in her dark, tired eyes.

She slowly wiped his face with a wet washcloth.

He had been in and out of consciousness for the past few days, but she had stayed vigilant by his bedside willing the infection from his head wound, and the subsequent fever to leave his weary body.

"Alex? ", the beautiful young woman leaning over him whispered, "It's me, Lydia."

"Lydia...?" he queried as he searched his foggy brain for answers, and found nothing but emptiness.

"It's me, oh, Alex, it's me!" she said laughing as tears of happiness flowed down her face.

"This is a miracle! God has brought you back to me!"

She ran her fingers through his thick dark hair, and placed a kiss on his unsuspecting lips.

"Lydia?" managed to croak out.

"Yes, my love?" she whispered.

"Lydia...who are you?"

Lydia stared down in horror as Alex's words washed over her.

Who was she?

Had the four years on the battlefield completely erased all his memories of her?

Surely not!

Had this war-ravaged weary soldier seen so much that he had returned broken in both body and spirit? She shuddered as she thought of so many men who had been sent home in such a state. Their bodies may have been returned to their families, but their stricken gaze belied the fact that they had lost their spirit out on the battlefront.

'Dear God, Not my Alex!' she felt her heart cry out.

She had been through so much heartache. He had suffered so much pain. They had faced insurmountable odds, but God had given them the strength needed to press on.

After all they had been through, Lydia was not about to give up now!

She pulled a small wooden stool up to the side of Alex's sickbed, and sat down. Praying for patience, Lydia reached for Alex's hand, and slowly began to fill in the missing pieces of his life.

The following morning, Alex opened his eyes just as the rising sun peeked through the window of the small bedroom where he lay.

His fever had finally dissipated, and

Alex awoke feeling refreshed.   He was finally on the mend.

His head swirled with the details of his life that Lydia had shared with him the previous evening.

"Lydia."

Just the sight of her took his breath away, and made his heart hammer a staccato in his chest. With her creamy, pale skin, and dark raven hair, she was the most beautiful creature he had ever seen.

Even more incredulous was the fact that she was his fiancé!

How he wished with all his heart that his memory would return so he could remember her!

With that sobering thought, Alex realized what he must do as soon as he was able. Lydia was in love with a man who had perished long ago. The Alex she knew, and loved was no more.
Replaced by an empty shell of a man.

A man who hadn't even known his own name!

Lydia woke, and quickly dressed.

The events surrounding the past month had left her breathless.

Her Alex had returned!

Daily she had gone to the home of Julia MacIntosh to care for the poor sick man whom she loved with her whole heart.

Daily, she had prayed for God's healing and restoration, but Alex's memories had not returned. His mind had been wiped as clean as a blank slate.

Daily, Mickey had transported her to and from the MacIntosh home. Whether she needed a listening ear or a comforting hug, he was there for her. Alex's care was both physically and emotionally draining, and countless times, Lydia found herself thanking God for sending Mickey into her life to lend her the support she needed.

Mickey was a good man with a good heart, and he, too, had become an integral part of her life.

Quickly combing her long tresses, Lydia slipped into her long coat, and laced up her boots. Although the sun provided warmth later in the day, a winter chill still lingered in the early April mornings.

Today was the day!

Without any clues as to why Alex had been mistakenly told he was Corporal MacIntosh, Alex had decided to return to his boyhood home to try and piece together the life he had lost.

Lydia, too, was leaving behind her Aunt, and Uncle's lavish Toronto home, and once again returning to her families' century old farmhouse.

Like a jigsaw puzzle, the broken pieces of her life were slowly falling into place. Only one thing saddened her.

Lydia knew she would miss Mickey more

than she would ever let on.

Chapter Seventeen

   The horse drawn carriage bumped and
rattled down the winding dirt road, but
Lydia didn't seem to notice.
   Nearly a year had passed since that
fateful day when Lydia had received the
awful news that her Alex had perished.
She had left her hometown an empty,
bitter woman, but was returning vibrant,
full of life, and best of all, her Alex
was with her!
   They passed the little schoolhouse,
and she smiled as she saw the children
frolicking in the yard in the warm,
noontime sun.
   Continuing on, they passed the little
country church she had attended her
whole life. The minister was sweeping
the front step, and he waved as they
passed.
   Yes it was good to be home!
   Rounding the bend, Lydia saw the
sparkling lake. Her mind flew back to
the night her Alex had proposed. There
had been ice on the lake then, and
couples were slowly skating on the
shimmering surface. It had been a
magical night, and the love that shone
in Alex's eyes had left her breathless.
He had been willing to let her go to

save her from heartache, but she had refused.

Obstinate as ever, she had chosen her path, and it was one she would never regret.

The weeks flew by, and soon May was upon them.

Flowers blossomed, and the birds sang of new beginnings.

It was a season of joy, but for Alex there was only confusion.

He had struggled to find his place in his real family. His parents had been so supportive, and his younger sister, Elizabeth, had done all she could to ease the transition, but he could see in their eyes that coping with his loss was hard on them as well.

How hard it must be to have a son and brother who could not remember their years together before the war had torn them apart!

How awful to have to be reintroduced to family as though they were strangers, for indeed, to Alex's empty mind they were.

Lydia was another story.

Beautiful, and vibrant, Alex found himself captivated by her every move. Her face shone with her love for him. Hope and joy reflected in all she would do.

She was happy, but Alex was not.

Lydia encouraged him to remember any chance she got. She spoke of the past as if it were the present, and expected him to follow.

He could not.

She remembered a world, and a time forever lost to him.

He had hoped his return home would reopen to him the scattered remnants of his memories, but instead, he was overcome with emptiness.

With no hope of ever regaining his consciousness, Alex turned his anger and frustration towards another source.

Lydia.

He was not the same man, nor would he ever be.

This was the present.

The past was gone, and now it was time to make some decisions about the future.

Mickey couldn't help the smile that made its way across his face.

After a long, hard day at work, he was rewarded with a letter in the mail from Lydia. He settled down on a worn, wooden bench out front of the Post Office, and began to read:

Dearest Mickey;

Sorry it has taken me so long to write, but I thought it best to get settled in first.

Alex is managing quite well, but

things are not going as I had hoped.
Frustration has changed him into another
man-one I do not know.

My heart aches for my Alex, and I fear
he is forever gone.

I see no love in his eyes, only pain,
and anger, and I wonder what is to
become of our future.

Are we even meant to be together?

It is a question I have dared not
utter till now for fear of what the
answer may be.

Once I thought I knew what my future
held, but now I am so unsure.

Is this God's Plan? That too is a
question that haunts me.

My heart is aching, and I feel my
strength waning. How much longer I can
stand this, I do not know.

I pray for answers, for hope, and for
peace, but I have found none.

I miss you, dear friend.

I wish you were here so that I could
once again discuss face to face what I
am even now experiencing. You are wise
beyond your years, and I miss your kind
heart, and caring words of advice.

I trust all is well with you, and you
are in good health.

May God be with you, my friend.

Sincerely,

Lydia Thompson

Mickey read, and reread the short
letter.

How he missed Lydia!

He had grown so close to this dear woman, and even now he felt himself reconsidering his former resolve. Maybe THIS was God's plan!

There was only one way to tell.

Mickey quickly made his way home, and packed his bags. With a loving pat on the head, he left his furry companion, Scrap, with a neighbor, and made his way to the train station. There he purchased a ticket, and boarded a train...

Chapter Eighteen

Lydia was just clearing the dishes from the supper table when she was startled by a firm knock on the old wooden front door. She was even more surprised when she opened it and saw a familiar face.

"Mickey!" she exclaimed as she gave him a warm hug.

How good it was to see her dear friend once again!

Alex watched the friendly exchange from the parlor, and knew what he must do. There was no use pretending.

Alex WAS dead.

Maybe there wasn't a cross to mark the place he had lost the happy life he had lived, but he was gone just the same.

All that remained were memories-His family's memories of his boyhood days and Lydia's memories of an undying love.

Sadly, that love had died the day Alex had lost himself.

It was time to bury the past.

"Lydia, can we please talk?" Alex motioned Lydia to the ornate settee beside him.

Lydia nodded and sat beside him.

The past few days had been a flurry of excitement as Lydia and Alex had showed Mickey all the wonderful things their little town had to offer.

Lydia had been so happy and carefree since Mickey's visit, and that had strengthened Alex's resolve even more.

Alex was a man of honor.

He was loyal and faithful, and he knew the beautiful girl he had asked to share his life was the same.

She would never betray his love, but he would set her free. It was time to do what he had put off for far too long.

"Lydia, I wish to end our engagement"

Stunned silence followed his statement, and one could have heard a pin drop upon the polished hardwood floors.

Lydia's eyes shone with tears as Alex's words penetrated her senses,

"You are in love with a man who once was. We are living in the past, and relishing a love that we once had.

That love died in the War.

I am so sorry, dear girl. You have been so faithful and have been beside me through this horrible ordeal, but the time has come to move on. I can not and will not hold you hostage to this engagement.

Go and live your life. You are free to become the wife and mother you were meant to be"

His words were firm, but Lydia could see the pain behind the mask.

She reached for him, but he rose hastily and headed for the door.

"We need a clean break, Lydia" he said as he paused with his hand on the door knob. His voice choked on the emotion of what he knew he must do to force her to move on.

"For this to work, I think it best if we not see each other anymore.

I can never repay you for all you have done for me.

May God be with you, and grant you a happy fulfilling life" And with that he disappeared into the night.

With a sob, Lydia sank back onto the settee and let the realization slowly dawn on her that she was now a free woman.

This battle between past and present that she had fought for too long finally had a winner.

The present had emerged victor.

This was not the fairytale she had dreamed.

Her life had been full of mountain top experiences, but with it had come avalanches that had threatened to crush her very existence.

Somehow she had always survived. But that survival had ultimately cost her a life without the one thing that she treasured most.

Alex and Lydia Thorne would never, ever be.

Chapter Nineteen

Summer turned to fall, but the colorful array of the autumn leaves did nothing to brighten downtrodden spirits.

Crisp and brisk and as unforgiving as the war, which had stolen a young and tender romance, the winter was soon upon them with a vengence. Snow swirled, and the bitter cold kept even the most daring of souls close to the warmth of the fire.

Then almost as quickly as it had come, the winter had past.

Lydia watched the as the birds outside her window chirped merrily as they built their nests. They were so beautiful, and so free.

Free.

Alex had set her free. It had been a heartbreaking experience and one she was still reeling from.

Now, nearly a year later she had slowly begun to pick up the pieces of her shattered life.

Mickey had been there to help. Although she knew that Alex alone held the key to her heart, her and Mickey had grown close.

Mickey was a good man-strong, hard working, trustworthy and He loved God above all else. She treasured their friendship.

Alex had asked for a clean break. Lydia had respected his wishes, packed her bags, and returned with Mickey to her Uncle's lavish Toronto home.

Sunny Brook Convalescent Care Center had been glad to hire her on once again, and, slowly, like the soldiers within its walls, Lydia had begun to mend.

She had befriended many of the residents, doctors and nurses and had surrounded herself with people with sunny dispositions like the ginger-hair nurse, Carolyn Johnson.

"Good morning, Sunshine" Mickey's jovial laugh broke into her sullen thoughts, "Today is a good day!"

"Yes it is" Lydia's smile warmed the room as she turned from the window, and reached for her large, beaded hand bag "Today I pick up that gorgeous, lace wedding dress from my favorite seamstress!"

Mickey groaned in mock dismay as he took her bag, and followed her out the door and to his waiting carriage.

Alex led his horse over to the hitching post in front of the old General Store, and glanced over at the few elderly men who lingered deep in conversation by the door.

Some would have called them gossips, but here in this small town, there was no such thing as a local newspaper and stories were passed by word of mouth. Amongst the graying heads, Alex noticed Lydia's father and ducked his head as he walked briskly past them and into the store.

Alex had brought shame to himself in both his and Lydia's families eyes when he had severed their relationship.

No one seemed to care that he had no recollection of her or their long lost love.

In this tiny town, their love had been written in stone.

People had watched them play as children, and eventually fall in love. They lived for the fairytale. But Alex's fairytale had a twisted ending.

Hastily, he gathered together the few

supplies he had come for, and nodded his head at the men by the door who lifted their heads to stare as he passed.

He was untying his horse as he overheard Lydia's father mention her name, and he paused for a moment longer then necessary to eavesdrop on the man's conversation.

"The wedding is next week, and Lydia is so excited. We are so happy for them" he was saying. "Sadly, me and the wife are unable to attend as she has been ill as of late and too weak to travel"

"Such a shame" said another neighbor-a short stout man with a gravelly voice "Would have been nice to see them get hitched there in the big city"

"For sure" Lydias father agreed "But the bride and groom are planning on visiting at Christmas time..." his voice trailed off as he and the other men entered the store.

Alex turned away.

He couldn't help but feel a tad disappointed in the fact that Lydia had finally moved on without him.

Sadness overwhelmed him as he untied his horse, mounted and turned him towards home.

He had taken the high road and set Lydia free, but was she ever really his if she could marry another in less then a year?

Chapter Twenty

The setting sun outlined the silhouette of the future bride and groom.

Hands clasped, they paused to gaze at the beautiful cathedral where they would marry in just a few short days. Life had been rough, the war had been hard, but God had brought them together-of this they were sure.

No matter what the future held, they would face it together.

Alex gazed at himself in the small mirror hanging over the wash basin with a razor in hand.

The once handsome, chiseled features were now masked beneath a thick furry mass. The scruffy whiskers that he had been hiding behind since his breakup with Lydia last year needed to go!

He raised the razor and began to shave.

Slowly the thick mass fell away and was replaced by a face bearing the marks of a man who had seen the thick of battle. A scar still snaked its way across his left cheek, and his eyes that once danced in happiness bore a great empty sadness.

Such was Alex Thorne.

The boy who had become a man seemingly

overnight for his country.   The one who
had sacrificed all he once held dear.
The one who's mind had become a blank
slate and all that was left was to pick
up the chalk and once again begin to
write.

Alex laid down the razor, and picked
up the clean facecloth and wiped it
across his face. As he did, he noticed
that he had knicked himself shaving.

He peered closer into the mirror to
survey the damage.

A crimson trickle seeped its way out
of the tiny wound and wound its way
downward.

Blood.

Instantly Alex's house was transformed
into a battlefield.

There was blood-so much blood!

People were crying out. Pain and
suffering was everywhere.

A dying Chuck MacIntosh was pressing
dog tags into Alex's hands. He slipped
them into his trouser pockets but the
heat was too unbearable. He yanked off
his own and threw them into the inferno
as the roof crashed around him.

He must get away!

His head throbbed and he stumbled
blindly towards the door. He yanked it
open, and dashed into the barn.

There was no time to saddle up-he must
escape now!

He climbed bareback onto his trusty horse, and urged him into a full gallop.

Past the schoolhouse he raced, and he could hear the sweet voice of the teacher as she taught her eager students.

He did not pause as the church came into view, but his ears echoed with the now silent refrain of a Christmas carol from a bygone year.

Only when he reached the pond did he reign his horse to a stop. Surrounded by a few barefoot boys with fishing rods in hand, Alex saw only the swirling snow, and a frozen skating rink with happy couples.

He dismounted from his now panting steed, and for the first time since the war, he remembered the dear girl to who he had pledged his undying love to in this very spot. The love had shone in her eyes that night and had made his heart melt within his chest as she promised to marry him and be his forever.

"Lydia!" he breathed heavily as the scene faded, and he realized he was standing perilously close to the edge of an open pond.

"God help me! What have I done?" he lamented.

He fell to his knees as the past few years sorted itself out in his troubled brain.

"Please God, have it not be too late!"

Lydia's father had said she was to be
married this very week!

Without Lydia, his life would be
empty.

Too late he had realized just what she
had meant to him. He should have gotten
to know her once again for surely
falling in love with such a girl would
have been easy to do twice!

Why had he been so stubborn?

Why had he set her free?

Without stopping even to pack, Alex
raced to the station and bought a ticket
on the next train to Toronto. Luckily,
it was just preparing to leave that very
afternoon.

Alex left his horse at the stables in
town, and boarded the train with a heavy
heart.

As it pulled out of the station with a
puff of smoke, he had a sinking feeling.

He would never make it in time.

Chapter Twenty One

Today was the day!

Lydia jumped out of her luxurious bed
with a smile on her face and glanced
around the spacious room she had called
home for nearly a year.

Truly, her Aunt and Uncle had been

blessed with prosperity, and she had
been lucky that they had opened their
home to her.

She pulled open the huge ornate
armoire and gazed in admiration at the
beautiful lace creation in front of her.
She let her fingers trail over the silk
bodice and closed her eyes.

In just a few short hours, this dress
would be worn by a glowing bride as she
marched down the aisle to meet her
friend, and confidant-the one to whom
she would pledge her heart and promise
to love for as long as she had breath.

To wear such a wedding dress had
always been Lydia's dream!

Lydia's thoughts were interrupted as
the large clock on the mantle chimed
nine times.

Her dear friend, and co-worker,
Carolyn Johnson, would be here to begin
preparations with her at any moment, and
Lydia still had so much to do.
Slowly, she closed the enormous doors
and turned away from the beautiful
dress.

The train had barely come to a stop
when Alex bounded off.

It was only eleven in the morning, but
already the warm sun beat down
threatening a scorcher of a late spring
day.

Momentarily blinded by the light, he

glanced around in confusion before darting into the small station house to ask for directions to the street where Lydia had been living with her Uncle Herb and Aunt Bertha.

A few short minutes later, he emerged, map in hand.

Hailing a taxi, he whispered a prayer that he was not already too late.

The enormous Thompson home loomed in all its majesty in the suburbs just outside the city of Toronto.

Alex raced up the stone walkway, and lifted the heavily carved knocker on the massive wooden doors.

As he stepped back, he could hear a grandfather clock deep within the house begin to chime twelve times.

It was noon.

The door swung open and a raven-haired maid with a crisp white apron smiled at him.

"Yes sir?" she inquired politely

"Is Lydia home?" Alex heard himself say in a shaky voice.

In his hurry to get here, he had failed to go over what he would say once he saw her again. All that had mattered was that he arrive in time!

"I'm so sorry, sir" the maid said, "She is not. She left for the wedding over an hour ago."

"What church?" asked Alex impatiently

despite the fact that he remembered
hearing the clock announce it was
already twelve.

   He prayed the church was not far away!

   "Its being held at The Lighthouse
Cathedral" the woman said
"But you will never make it in time,
Sir.
The wedding started at noon."

Chapter Twenty Two

   The Thompson Wedding was to be a
beautiful affair and friends and family
had come from far and wide to see the
union of the glowing young bride and her
ruggedly handsome husband.

   Glancing around the crowded church,
Lydia felt a twinge of sadness engulf
her at the thought of her own parents
being unable to attend.

   Her mother's health had not been good
as of late, and Lydia resolved to return
home for a visit sooner rather then
later. Family had become such an
integral part of her life since the War.

   Now adorned in the gorgeous gown, the
bride, waiting patiently at the back of
the church, ran her fingers lightly over
the material.

   The shell bodice was covered in pearl
sequins and flowed outward into yards of
ivory lace and white silk.

   It was a dress to be admired.

As the music played softly, Lydia slowly walked down the long aisle, past the row upon row of wooden pews, and pausing only for only a moment before joining those already at the altar.

A smile lit her face and she stifled a laugh as she caught a glance of Mickey looking all stuffy in a suit standing at the altar and grinning mischievously back at her.

He stepped forward, gave her his arm, and led her to her place.

Such a gentleman!

Trying to keep her composure, she glanced down at the beautiful bouquet that she held in her hands.

This wedding was beautiful and no expense had been spared.

Her Uncle was a generous man, and he had insisted on paying for everything. This bride was family he had said and he would make sure she had the wedding of her dreams.

It was like a fairytale.

"Do you take this man to be your husband...As long as you both shall live…Till death do you part?"

There was no hesitation.

"I do"

Guests streamed out of the vast cathedral and into the afternoon sun. Although beautiful, the massive stone cathedral had a chilly dampness to it in early spring and the warmth of the sun was a welcome reprieve.

The beautiful bride, her face alight with happiness, stood with her groom on the steps and greeted all the well-wishers as they passed.

It was the happiest of occasions!

Mickey and Lydia stood side by side watching the crowd file by, and shaking the hands of the happy throng.

No one seemed to notice the taxi that came to a halting stop in front of the emptying cathedral.

Nor did they notice the somewhat disheveled man that exited and bounded towards the stone steps as though his very life hung in the balance (for indeed in Alex's now opened eyes it did!).

It was only when Alex had pushed through the crowd that he saw the duo. He watched as Mickey leaned towards Lydia, and Lydia threw her head back and laughed merrily.

And even as he felt hope and despair play a tug of war with his heart, Alex caught sight of the stunning ivory lace dress with the pale rose colored sash that Lydia wore.

Mickey stood gallantly beside her in a neatly pressed suit with a look of happiness across his face.

"Dear God,no!" Alex cried out in

despair as he halted a few feet from the
love of his life.
    "I am too late!"

Chapter Twenty Three

    "Alex?"
    Lydia's query came out in a hoarse
whisper as she stepped forward and gazed
in shock at the figure in front of her.
    Her Alex had been a boy, but this was
a man.
    His handsome face had been marked by a
cruel, long war, but it had not dimmed
the life within.
    Even gazing at him now, she could see
the emotion in his eyes. Was it love
that she saw springing from its very
depths?
    Surely not!
    This was Alex-the man she had pledged
to become one with-the one who had held
her very heart in the palm of his hand.
That heart had beaten for him alone, but
he had done the unthinkable and crushed
it.
    One could not really blame the man for
trying to do the correct thing. After
all, Alex had no recollection of their
lives before the accident nor could he
recall their love.
    He had done what he thought was right.
    He had set Lydia free. Free to live

her life without him. Free to marry another.
And now here they were standing on the church steps.

'Hopelessness'
That was the only word that could describe how Alex felt at that very moment as he gazed at the woman of his dreams resplendent in a gorgeous dress on the church steps following her wedding with another man.

He couldn't help but feel the jealousy spring up within him as he gazed at Mickey O'Dell.

What a lucky man!

He hoped and prayed Mickey would treat Lydia with the love, and respect she deserved!

And to think, had he not been a fool and released her from her commitment, this might have been him standing here today...

Resolved to be the better man, Alex attempted to regain his composure, and offered his hand to the friendly face of the man standing in front of him who had been there for Lydia when he had failed.

"Congratulations on your wedding, Mickey. Lydia is a wonderful woman and you, sir, are a very blessed man.

I wish you both all the happiness life has to offer" his voice choked with emotion on the last words, and he quickly turned away and fled before he completely lost his composure.

His life had ended.

His dreams had been crushed.

He had nothing left but to go home and attempt to put the jigsaw puzzle of his life back together.

But somehow, deep within, he knew that without Lydia, that puzzle would always have a missing piece.

"Alex, wait!"

The words were breathless as Lydia rushed to his side.

He had attempted to make a speedy exit around the side of the church and into the gardens so he could regain his composure enough to leave past the lingering guests who were casting strange looks in his direction after his hurried, disheveled appearance.

He paused underneath the spreading limbs of an old apple tree which had begun to blossom early due to the unusually warm weather they had experienced as of late.

"Alex, do you remember me?

Do you remember us?"

Tears streamed unbidden from his eyes as he slowly nodded.

"I do, Lydia. God help me, I do!

But I remembered too late!

What we had must forever be put behind us..."

"Whatever do you mean? It is never too late! I love you and I always will!"

"It was not meant to be" Alex said "You are married to Mickey now. God brought you two together amidst all the pain and suffering that you experienced.

I wish you both all the best life has to offer, dear girl"

"What? How?" Lydia asked incredulously,

"Mickey and I are not married! Whoever told you such a thing?"

"But, the wedding...the beautiful dress…"

"Was for my cousin, Louie Thompson! He married my dear friend and co-worker, Carolyn Johnson today!

I was the maid of honor, and my good friend, Mickey, the best man!"

"So...You are still free?" Alex asked hopefully. Lately he had hated that word with a passion, now it was the one thing he needed to hear.

Lydia nodded, and Alex dared to press on.

Too much time had passed.

Too much had gone wrong, but God had worked it all for good.

It was now or never.

He dropped to one knee beneath the swaying boughs of the fragrantly blossomed tree, and gently took her hand in his as he gazed deeply into her eyes.

The emotion was overwhelming as he spoke:

"Lydia Thompson, in a world full of uncertainty of one thing I am sure, you are the love of my life.

I believe with all my heart that God has brought us together.

Will you do me the honor of becoming my wife and trusting that no matter what the future holds, we can face it together?"

Without a moment's hesitation, and with tears streaming down her cheeks, Lydia whispered

"Yes, Alex, my love, I would be honored to be your wife, and to walk through life by your side."

Her face radiated all the love and joy that she had held locked away as Alex swept her into his arms and kissed her passionately.

Like a bird released from its cage, her spirit took flight.

She was finally free.

Free to love.

Free to be who she was meant to be-the Mrs. Alex Thorne.

And Alex's puzzle had finally found it's missing piece.

The End

SCARLET IBIS JAMES

Love In The Dark: A Holiday Romance For Grown-Ups

From The Author of Scarlet Yearnings Comes a New Short Story of Winter Nights and Second Chances

DISCOVERY AND KEY, NEW YORK
A SUBSIDIARY OF DKJ ENTERPRISES

Love in the Dark
A Holiday Romance for Grown-Ups.

First published by DKJ Enterprises LLC 2025

For information, please email the publisher at publisher@dkj-e.com.

ISBN-13: 979-8-9993829-2-4